P9-CDS-610

Little Loon and Papa

Toni Buzzeo

illustrated by
Margaret Spengler

DIAL BOOKS FOR YOUNG READERS
New York

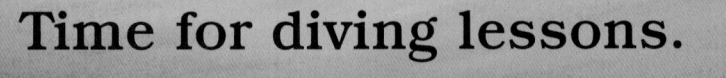

Papa Loon calls
to his timid Little Loon:

HOO
  HOO   HOO
    HOO   HOO
          HOO

Time for diving lessons.

Oh, no.
Little Loon backs away.
But Papa dips Little Loon's head down.
And Papa tips Little Loon's tail up.

Little Loon wobbles back flat.

Little Loon watches Papa
SQUEEZE air out,
TUCK his feathers tight,
and—*ZIP!*—
disappear from sight.

Little Loon quivers
and watches and waits
until he spots
Papa's sharp bill.

Again—
Papa Loon
dips him
and tips him.
But Little Loon wobbles back flat.

SQUEEZE,
TUCK,
ZIP!
Papa disappears from sight.

Quick-quick
Little Loon kick-kicks
away from
Papa's diving lessons.

But at the weedy shore—

*SPLASH, DRIP,
HRROOOOO!*

Little Loon spots
great, bony legs
and a wide antler rack
with weeds dripping down.

peep peep
Where is Papa?

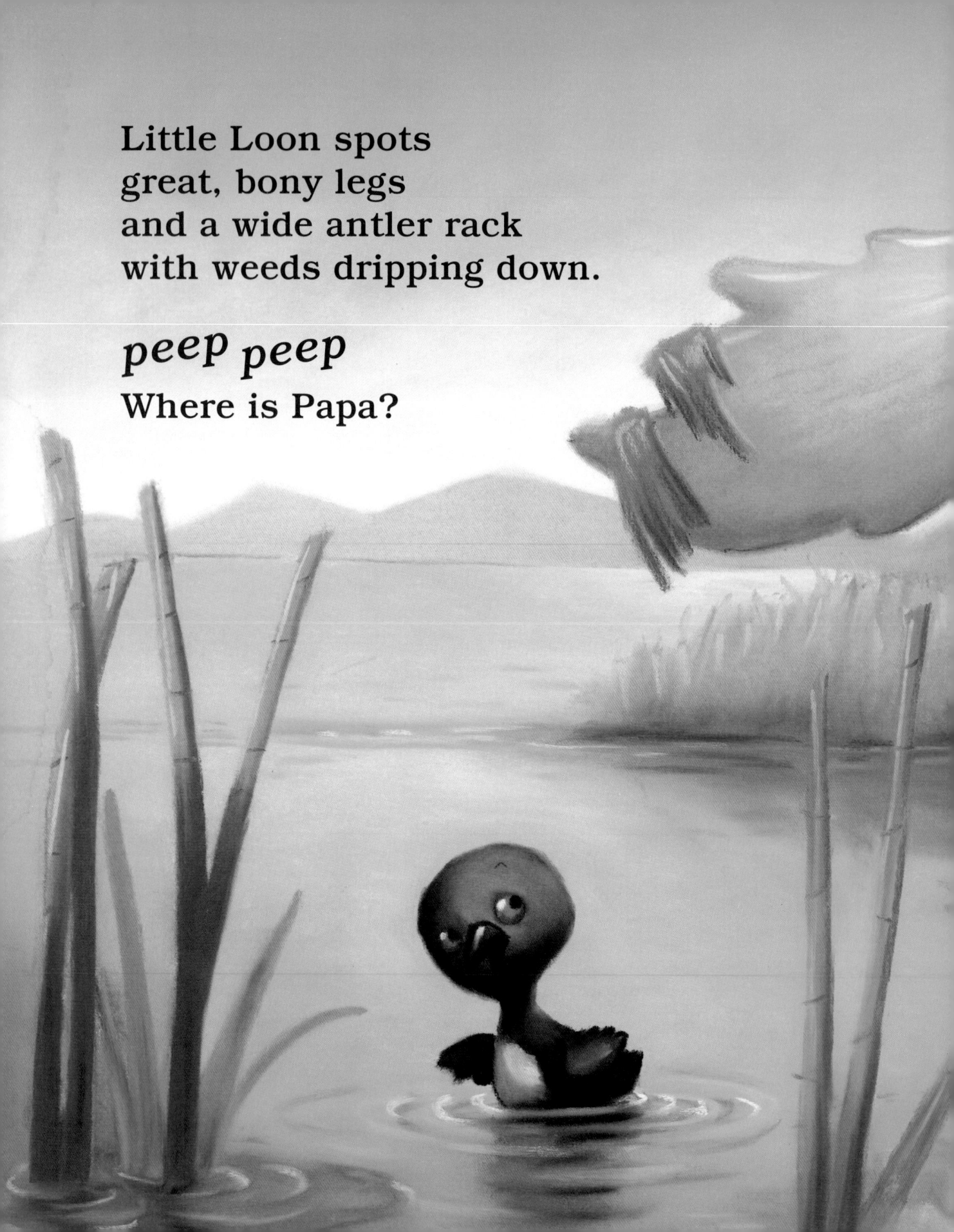

Little Loon zigzags toward the rocks, but—

GRUFFLE, SNUFFLE, GROWL!

Little Loon spots
a great, shaggy face
and a wide brown snout
with a trout hanging out.

peep peep
Where is Papa?

Gliding smoother,
a little like Papa,
he swims as fast as he can,
until—

WHACK,

WHAP,

CRASH!

Little Loon spots
a great, broad tail
and wide front teeth
with bark sprinkling down.

peep peep peep peep!
Where is Papa?

Then he hears:

AHA-OOO-OOOO'OOOO-OOO-AHHH!

Little Loon spins.
Little Loon flaps.
Little Loon backs away.
Then, Little Loon tries.

He SQUEEZES air out
and TUCKS in his fluff.
He WIGGLES his feet,
he WAGGLES his wings,
and—*PLUNK!*—
disappears from sight.

When his head pops up—
There's Papa!

HOO
HOO
HOO
HOO
HOO
HOO
HOO

calls Papa.

Papa splash-paddles
close to his Little Loon,
offers a treat
from his long, sharp bill,
and tucks Little Loon
snug under his wing.

To the High Test Girls, without whose abiding love and belief,
I might never have learned to dive—T.B.

To my son, Matthew,
the best little boy in the whole world—M.S.

Published by Dial Books for Young Readers
A division of Penguin Young Readers Group
345 Hudson Street
New York, New York 10014

Text copyright © 2004 by Toni Buzzeo
Illustrations copyright © 2004 by Margaret Spengler
All rights reserved
Designed by Kimi Weart
Text set in Bookman
Manufactured in China on acid-free paper
5 7 9 10 8 6 4

Library of Congress Cataloging-in-Publication Data
Buzzeo, Toni.
Little Loon and Papa / Toni Buzzeo ; illustrated by Margaret Spengler.
p. cm.
Summary: Motivated by a challenging situation and his supportive father,
Little Loon finally learns to dive.
ISBN 0-8037-2958-8
[1. Swimming—Fiction. 2. Father and child—Fiction. 3. Loons—Fiction.
4. Animals—Fiction.] I. Spengler, Margaret, ill. II. Title.
PZ7.B9832Li 2004
[E]—dc21   2003003530

Special thanks to Kate Taylor of the Loon Preservation Committee for
her guidance on loon calls and illustration details—T.B.

The art was created using pastels.
Special Markets ISBN 978-0-8037-3130-1
Not For Resale

This Imagination Library edition is published by Penguin Group (USA), a Pearson
company, exclusively for Dolly Parton's Imagination Library, a not-for-profit
program designed to inspire a love of reading and learning, sponsored in part by The
Dollywood Foundation. Penguin's trade editions of this work are available wherever
books are sold.